The Secret Place

RACHEL ROONEY

Cover Illustration by Josh Gray

Fulton Books, Inc.
Meadville, PA

Published by Fulton Books 2021

ISBN 978-1-63985-387-8 (paperback)
ISBN 978-1-63985-388-5 (digital)

Printed in the United States of America

To everyone who thinks they might not be able to do something, you can do anything you set your mind to.

Acknowledgments

Thanks to Adela, Keira, Ellie, Maggie, Zoey, Grandma, Grandpa, Cigi, and Mom for being the test readers of this book. Thanks to Josh for doing my amazing cover illustration. Mrs. Brooks for having us read many different genres that helped me figure out how to write a chapter book. Thanks to Dad for helping me make such good cliff-hangers. This story was inspired by one of my dreams.

Chapter 1

Hi, my name is Ali, and I am one of the girls that live at Miss Jewel's House for Girls. Here are some things you need to know. Haley and Lily are my best friends, and we all don't like Rebecca. This is where our story starts.

"Can you believe how mean they are to us?" I ask.

"Ali, it is okay. Remember, we don't pay any attention to them," Haley says.

"I know, but sometimes they get on my nerves."

"I know, but we can't let them," Haley says.

"What happened?" Lily asks.

"Well, Rebecca and her gang knocked into us and said, 'Like sorry, I didn't see you there,'" I answer.

Lily says, "I know, they are mean to you, me, and Haley, but we just have to ignore them even though it is hard."

*****

Here comes Rebecca, and she asks, "Hey, guys, what's up?" Haley, Lily, and I all wonder if she was just being nice to us. Just so you know, Rebecca is another girl at Miss Jewel's House for Girls. She is really mean to us, but Miss Jewel adores Rebecca because she is so much like her.

"Anyway," Rebecca says, "if any of you want to be part of my group, you can start being more like me and that is how you can get in."

"Rebecca, we are not going to abandon our group to join yours," I say.

"Okay, that's fine with me. I didn't even want you in my group, anyway."

So I say to Haley and Lily, "Right, we will never abandon our group to go to Rebecca's."

Haley and Lily reply, "Right, friends forever stick together."

"Girls, we have some new girls here. Please come and meet them," Miss Jewel says.

All of us girls say, "Yes, Miss Jewel."

"Girls, I would like you to meet Emma, Olivia, and Isabelle," Miss Jewel says.

"Hi," Rebecca says. "If you are classy, then you want to be in my group. If you're not, then Ali's group would be for you."

"Miss Jewel, why do we have so many girls arriving at once?" I ask.

"Well, they are triplets," Miss Jewel replies.

"Oh, girls, just so you know, we are going to London tomorrow. So you might not want to unpack quite yet. Remember that everyone has to be packed by tomorrow. I am talking to you Ali, Haley, and Lily. Also, remember wake up by 7:00 a.m. because we are leaving at 9:00 a.m. Okay, now get to bed," says Miss Jewel.

Chapter 2

It was morning, and we were supposed to wake up at 7:00 a.m. But it is already 7:05 a.m. I forgot to set my alarm, and I got what was coming to me. I wake up to freezing cold water being poured on me. I exclaim, "Ah! Who did that?" I should have known. When I sit up, I see Rebecca and her gang standing there, laughing holding a bucket. "Ha ha ha," I say. "Very funny."

"Girls, get ready now," says Miss Jewel.

I go over and see Haley and Lily. Haley says, "I was just about to wake you up and then they distracted us."

"We had better get ready to go. We do not want to be left here. Let's get on the bus," I say.

*****

"Girls, before we get on the bus, we are going to get breakfast here," says Miss Jewel.

When we go down to breakfast, everyone is already down there; and all of the seats are taken, so Haley, Lily, and I have to sit on the floor.

Guess what? You know the new girls, Emma, Olivia, and Isabelle, well they decided to sit on the floor with us, and Emma says, "I think that we should be in your group."

Then Olivia says, "We saw what Rebecca did to you this morning, and we do not want any part of being in that group."

"Well," I say, "welcome to the group!"

"Girls," Miss Jewel says, "we do not sit on the floor! We are at Miss Jewel's House for Girls where you learn to become ladies."

"Yeah, that is not happening unless we're on a business trip with you. If we are not ladies, then we would make you look bad. In return, you would make us clean this whole place for a year. We don't want to do that," I say.

"Okay, okay, let's get on the bus," Miss Jewel says.

Chapter 3

We get on the tour bus with a bathroom and everything because Miss Jewel likes to look official. Oh, and surprise, we get to sit in the back by the bathroom because Rebecca and her gang take the seats in the front.

"This is so unfair! We always get the worst seats and chores because Miss Jewel likes Rebecca and her group better than us," I exclaim. "Hey, if you want to join Rebecca's group because they get the perks we would understand," I tell Emma, Olivia, and Isabelle.

"Are you nuts? We do not want to be part of a group like that," replies Olivia.

"Well, then since you are joining the group, we need to tell you some things," Haley says.

"Like what?" Emma asks.

"Well, for one thing, how we get back at Rebecca," Lily says.

"Wait," says Isabelle. "You can get back at Rebecca? How do you do it without getting chores?"

"Well," I say, "we have had some practice, considering Haley, Lily, Rebecca, and I along with a few of her gang have been here for our whole lives."

"Wait," says Emma, Olivia, and Isabelle at the same time. "You have been here all of your life!"

"Yeah," reply Haley, Lily, and I. "So we have had a lot of time to learn how to get back at Rebecca."

"Well, back to the plan," I say. "First of all, we use our chores to our advantage because we make it look like a mistake."

"How?" asks Emma.

"Well, let's say we are taking the trash or dirty laundry out. We always try to pass by Rebecca," I say.

"Then," says Haley, "we always pretend to trip and 'accidentally' pour all of it on her."

Isabelle asks, "Don't you just get more chores?"

"You would think so, but if we do this when Miss Jewel is busy, which she usually is trying to get investors, we do it then and Rebecca can't go running to her for help," says Lily.

"Oh, look, here comes trouble," I say. Sure enough here comes Rebecca.

"So you have decided to join Ali's group, haven't you? Well, your loss. If you change your mind, meet us down by the lake by our chateau."

"There is no way that any of us are going to join your little gang," says Olivia.

"Okay, suit yourselves," says Rebecca.

"Ladies, we are going to get on a plane to London so here are your tickets," says Miss Jewel.

Chapter 4

We get on the plane and are all so glad that we don't have to sit with Rebecca. We are all sitting with each other. Haley, Lily, and I are sitting right across from Emma, Olivia, and Isabelle. During the flight, Miss Jewel comes to check on us, but other than that, we tell Emma, Olivia, and Isabelle more about what we do to get back at Rebecca. We have to text sometimes because we don't want everyone else on the plane hearing. Luckily, we all have phones.

When we get there, it is about noon. We have time to get to the chateau and explore a little. We have to go to bed early because the meeting with the investor is in the morning.

"Girls, I am going to the salon and won't be back until about 9:30 p.m. I want all of you girls in bed before I get back," says Miss Jewel.

"Well," I ask my friends, "what do you want to do?"

"Sorry, guys, but I have to go. I promised Miss Jewel I would get some pictures of the creek for her website," says Lily.

"Oh, that's fine," says Haley.

"What do the rest of us want to do?" asks Haley.

"I wonder why Miss Jewel would want pictures of the creek and why she just asked Lily?" I ask.

"Now, Ali, we know that Lily isn't lying. She wouldn't do that to us," says Haley.

"You're right," I say. "I saw that there was a park a little way away so maybe we could go there."

"Sounds good to us," says Emma, Olivia, and Isabelle.

After we get back from the park, Lily still isn't back. We all wonder where she is, but she can take care of herself, so we decide to go to bed.

Later that night, we all wake up to a loud sound and realize that the loud sound is coming from a blow horn. Haley and I go down to see what it is, and when we come down the stairs, we get covered in water and sparkles by someone who looks familiar.

When the lights come on, we cannot believe what we see. Rebecca is saying, "Good one, Lily. Welcome to the group!"

"Lily, how could you?" Haley and I both ask.

"How can you leave our group for them?"

"Sorry, guys, but I am sick of being the ones who get the worst chores. So I thought I would join Rebecca's group," replies Lily.

"I can't believe you," I say. "I thought we were best friends that we were in this together."

"Now, Ali, I am just as mad as you are, but Lily made her decision and she will have to live with it. Let's just go back upstairs," says Haley.

When we get back upstairs to our room, Emma asks, "What happened to you guys?"

"Apparently, Lily has decided to switch sides. She did this to us to get in the group," I reply.

"But I thought that you guys were best friends, and she's lived with you guys for all of your lives. Why would she do that?" asks Isabelle.

"I guess she was just sick of being the ones who get the worst chores, but I honestly thought that doing it together would make it alright," replies Haley.

"Now, I just remembered something," I say. "Our motto is 'friends forever stick together.'"

"Oh, we really like that," says Emma, Olivia, and Isabelle.

"Well," says Haley, "we should probably get to bed so we are rested for the meeting with the investor tomorrow."

"Yeah, you're right," I say. "Good night, guys."

Chapter 5

The next morning, we get up at eight, and apparently Lily has switched rooms. Now she is in Rebecca and her group's room. The meeting with the investor is at 10:00 a.m., but Miss Jewel wants us to be there extra early because she doesn't want us to be late.

When we go down to breakfast, we again have to sit on the floor. Apparently, Lily is sitting up with Rebecca and her group. She looks at us but then looks back and whispers something to Rebecca, and they start laughing. After breakfast, we get dressed in the clothes that Miss Jewel got for us. We go downstairs and find that we are the first ones down there, so we just wait.

*****

Miss Jewel says, "Girls, we will be leaving in ten minutes. Now, I wonder where Rebecca and her group are. Also, girls, remember to behave yourselves today." At precisely 9:00 a.m., Rebecca and the rest of her group are ready to go. We get in the limo that is driving us to the meeting.

We get to the meeting at 9:30 a.m. Miss Jewel says, "Okay, girls, you can explore, but I want you back here by 9:45 a.m. just to be safe."

"Okay, where do you want to go?" I ask.

"We should just go exploring," says Haley. "We should also make sure we start heading back at 9:40 a.m."

"Okay, that sounds good," I say.

We start going around, not really knowing where we are going, and I accidentally bump into someone. "Oh, I am so sorry," I say. "I didn't mean to bump into you. I just wasn't looking where I was going."

"Oh, it is fine. It was my fault too," says a boy I don't know.

"Well, sorry again, but I have to go. Bye," I say.

"Bye," he replies.

"Hurry! Ali, we have to go," shouts Haley. "Who was that?"

"I don't know," I reply.

"Well, let's go. It is almost time for the meeting," Haley says.

I look back and he is gone. I wonder why he is here; this definitely isn't a normal place for a kid to be running around, but technically we are doing the same thing.

We hurry back to the lobby, and we get there just in time. "Girls, where have you been? You are just lucky you made it on time," says Miss Jewel. We go into the office where we are meeting the investor.

A man around his thirties comes in and says, "Hello, my name is Mr. Stephens, and you must be Miss Jewel. Nice to meet you."

"Hello, we are very honored to be meeting you," replies Miss Jewel. Well the meeting goes on. We just sit there like we are ladies and do what we usually do.

Mr. Stephens then says, "I will invest in you if you take one more girl. There were these parents who dropped off a brother and a sister and left a lot of money and a note that says to take care of their kids. I put them in a good orphanage, but the kids there are bullying them. So we thought that we could move the girl to your place. So do you agree?"

"Yes, we agree. Will we get to meet the girl today?" Miss Jewel asks.

"As a matter of fact, you can meet her right now. You can meet the boy too because we thought that you could bring her home with you today. He wanted to say goodbye. We can let the kids meet them first while we sign some papers. Kids, or should I say ladies, this way," replies Mr. Stephens.

We all go into the next room, and sure enough, I see something that amazes me. So you remember that boy that I accidently bumped into. He is the brother of the girl that is coming to stay with us.

"You!" I exclaim.

"Well, hello again," he says back.

Chapter 6

"Do you guys know each other?" asks Rebecca.

"No," I say. "We just bumped into each other while we were walking around. I am Ali and this Haley, Emma, Olivia, and Isabelle. This is Rebecca."

"I can introduce us. Thank you very much," interrupts Rebecca. "Well, I am Rebecca. This is Lily, Ava, Sally, and Chloe."

"I am Brandon, and this is Blair," says Brandon.

"Nice to meet you," I say. "Also, I am so sorry for bumping into you earlier."

"That's fine. Also, will some of you promise to look after Blair while she stays with you. We haven't ever been apart," says Brandon.

"Oh, my friends and I can look after Blair, if that is okay with you?" I ask Blair.

"Yeah, sure," Blair replies.

"Okay, we will probably be going back to Salem in about a day," I say. "Also, what orphanage do you guys go to?" I ask.

"Oh, we go to London's House for Children," Brandon replies.

"Wait," says Rebecca. "My group and I can look after Blair for you."

"Actually," says Blair, "I think I trust Ali more since my brother knows her and everything. Also, she seems nicer."

"How old are you, little girl?" asks Rebecca. "Because we are all teenagers. I think we have better judgment."

"For your information," Brandon replies, "she is ten and I agree with her judgment. Ali does seem nicer."

"Everything going alright here?" asks Mr. Stephens.

"Yes," we all reply.

"Well," he says, "can Blair and Brandon say their goodbyes because you will be going home tomorrow."

"Yes," Brandon and Blair both say.

After Mr. Stephens returns to the other room, Blair cries. "I don't want to leave you even though Ali and her friends seem nice."

"It's okay. We can still talk over the phone and video call. Don't worry. Ali will take good care of you," Brandon replies. "Ali," he asks, "can I talk to you in private for a minute?"

"Sure," I reply.

We go over away from the others while my friends comfort Blair. "You know that we have never been apart. Right?" he asks.

"Yeah, I know, and don't worry I will look after her for you. Trust me, I know what it is like," I reply.

"What do you mean by that?" Brandon questions.

"Well, Haley and I have been with Miss Jewel all of our lives, and Miss Jewel was seriously thinking of sending one of us to another orphanage. Trust me, we didn't want to get split up. We are like sisters since we have been at Miss Jewel's for all of our lives together. I get what she would be going through. Don't worry. First of all, my group will take great care of her, and second, you picked the right group. Is that all?" I ask.

He is just staring at me but eventually says, "Yeah, thanks!"

"No problem," I reply.

We head back over, and Haley asks me, "What was that about?"

"Oh, nothing. He was just making sure we take care of his little sister for him," I say.

Blair and Brandon say their goodbyes, and Brandon thanks us once more. After that, Miss Jewel and Mr. Stephens come back. Miss Jewel asks, "Ready to go, ladies?"

"Yep," we reply.

CHAPTER 6

All of us except Mr. Stephens and Brandon head for the door. Both Blair and I look back and wave at Brandon.

Chapter 7

When we get back to the chateau, we show Blair to our room. "Just a quick question." She asks, "Why aren't you and Rebecca friends, and do we go on these trips often?"

"To be fair," I say, "that was two questions, but yes, we go on at least one trip a month, and second of all, it is a long story, but here is the short clip. We both arrived at Miss Jewel's House for Girls, and Rebecca thought that it would be good to get Miss Jewel on her side. So she pretended that Haley, Lily, and I pushed her, and she hurt her ankle. After that, we got to do all the chores, and you know the rest."

Blair asks, "Okay, so when are we leaving to go back to Salem, Oregon?"

"We are supposed to be going to the airport at 10:00 a.m.," I say.

"Okay, also thanks for taking care of me," Blair replies.

"No problem," we all say to her.

Miss Jewel calls up to us, "Girls, we are having dinner. Come down, please."

"Coming," we all call back. When we get downstairs, of course, there is one seat left for Blair. So Haley, Emma, Olivia, Isabelle, and I sit on the floor.

"Why are Ali and her friends sitting on the floor?" asks Blair.

"Well," says Rebecca, "you see they aren't sophisticated enough to know that, that is not proper manners, which is why you should join our group."

"Or it could be that you and your group aren't sharing your seats with us, which makes you selfish," I fire back.

"Girls, let's not fight, considering it is Blair's first night with us," says Miss Jewel. We finish dinner in silence, but at the end of dinner, Miss Jewel says, "Girls, you had better go to sleep because we have to leave at 10:00 a.m. tomorrow. Good night, girls."

"Good night, Miss Jewel," we all reply.

*****

When we get upstairs, Blair says, "I am going to go call my brother."

"Okay, we'll just be in our room," says Emma.

"So what do you think of Brandon," Olivia asks me at once.

"What do you mean?" I ask.

"Well, it's obvious he likes you," Emma says.

"What? You guys must be crazy," I reply.

"No, it is you who's crazy. He trusted you more than Rebecca and stood up to that," says Isabelle.

"Yeah, because he was standing up to what his sister said. I mean would you really trust Rebecca?" I ask, totally confused now.

"Okay," says Haley, "but at least admit you think he is cute."

"What?" I reply. "Sure I think he is cute, and I think it was awesome that he stood up for his sister but—"

"But what?" Emma, Olivia, Isabelle, and Haley all ask.

"But I will never see him again, and I don't think he likes me," I say to all of them.

"He likes you. That part is definite," says Haley.

"Why didn't you do something about it?" asks Olivia.

"I didn't think he liked me, and I mean we just met," I say.

"Yeah, but you could have just said it," replies Isabelle.

"No way!" I exclaim. "That would be so weird, and what if he doesn't like me back?"

"Oh, trust us. He likes you," says Emma.

"Well, anyway, it's too late now," I say. "I think that Rebecca likes him. I mean did you see her trying to make him like her?"

"Yeah, but he doesn't like her," replies Haley.

"He likes you," says someone we don't know is standing there.

We all turn around and are so glad to see it is just Blair. "What?" we all ask.

"I said he likes you. He just told me and also said he wanted to meet me at the airport to say goodbye. So you could always tell him then," Blair suggests.

"But I don't want it to sound weird, and that would just be too fast. I mean we just met," I say.

"Yeah, my brother feels the same way, but one of you should tell each other because you won't see each other for at least a little while. Also, how old are you guys?" Blair replies.

"We are thirteen," I reply. "Haley and I actually have the same birthday on May 1st."

"Yep, my brother is also thirteen, but his birthday is on February 21st," Blair says.

"Okay, well, we should probably get to sleep since we have to wake up at eight tomorrow morning," I say. I really don't want to talk about this topic right now. I mean I do like him, but I feel like it would be weird if I just came out and said it.

I stay up until about midnight; I am about to fall asleep when I hear someone crying. I get up and realize that it is Blair. I go over and sit on the bed. I ask, "Hey, Blair, what's wrong?"

"This is the first night that my brother and I haven't been together." She sobs.

"Oh, okay, I understand, but it's okay. You can still talk to him and you have a picture, right? Why don't you look at it, and I am going to borrow your phone really quickly. Is that okay?" I ask. Blair nods.

I take her phone and put her brother's phone number on my contacts then I call him. He answers really quickly and says, "Who is it?" Apparently, Blair isn't the only one staying awake.

"Hi, this is Ali from earlier today. We met and Blair came with us," I say.

"Ali, is Blair okay? Is she hurt? Do I need to be there because I will run or ride the bus or anything?" he says.

"No, she's fine. She's just crying because she misses you," I reassure him.

"Okay, can I talk to her?" he asks.

"I was actually just going to suggest that," I say. "Here she is."

I give the phone to Blair and let her talk to her brother alone. After Blair gives me back the phone, I ask, "Is she okay now because I can do whatever she wants. If you know what to do to get her to sleep that would be great. I can get her whatever."

All I hear is silence, so then I say, "Hello, Brandon, are you still there?" I ask.

"Oh yeah, I am still here. If you could just stay with her, that would be great. Thanks," he says.

"Yeah, sure, I'll do that. Bye then and see you tomorrow," I say.

Brandon replies, "What? Oh, right, bye and see you tomorrow."

After I hang up, I go over to Blair and ask, "Hey, are you okay now?"

"Yeah, I'm fine and sorry for waking you up," she replies.

"Oh, Blair, it's okay. I want you to wake me up if you ever are sad or have a bad dream or you need anything, okay? We're like sisters now. We help each other," I say. "We should probably get you to sleep now. Okay?"

"Okay," she replies.

After I get Blair back to sleep, I think that I better go to sleep too. I go to my bed, and in what feels like two minutes, Haley wakes me up.

"Ali, Ali, Ali! It's time to get up, and you had better do it before you get ice cold water poured on you again."

"Thanks, Haley. I just had a long night," I reply.

"What do you mean?" asks Haley. "Didn't you sleep?"

"Yeah, a little, but I was up until midnight. Then I stayed awake until two in the morning, comforting and getting Blair back to bed," I reply.

"Oh, well, at least you can sleep on the plane ride home, but right now we have to get ready," Haley says.

"Okay, I'll be down in a minute," I say. I throw on something comfortable for the plane ride home and go downstairs. We eat really quickly, get in the van, and then head to the airport.

When we get there, Blair jumps out of the van and runs up to her brother. We all get out of the van and get our luggage. I do my best not to look over at Brandon, but he ends up coming over to me. He asks, "Could I talk to you for a minute over there?"

"Yeah, sure," I reply.

We walk over away from the rest of the group. "I just wanted to say thank you again for staying with Blair, and she told me she thinks of you as her big sister, so thank you," he says.

"Yeah, no problem. We all have to be in this together because we only have each other," I say. "Also, I have your number, and I might call you or Blair might call you using my phone. I just thought you should know."

"Yeah, so we might talk to each other more then?" he asks.

"Yeah, and I will take good care of Blair," I say. I am also thinking at the same time, *Just tell him, just tell him.*

Miss Jewel calls, "Ali, hurry up. We have to get up to boarding."

"Well, I have to go. Bye," I say.

"Bye," he says back.

Chapter 8

We are on the plane, and as soon as I sit down by Haley and Blair, I fall asleep. Next thing I know I am being awakened by cold ice water being thrown on me, and of course, when I open my eyes, I see Rebecca and Lily standing there with an empty bucket.

Next thing I know, I hear someone that kind of sounds like someone I know. Just it is a boy's voice and sure enough he's not here. Then I see who I never thought I would see on this plane. Now, I am totally awake, and I ask, "What are you doing here?" But I take a closer look and see that he is in a disguise. Also, if you haven't realized who I am talking about, it is Brandon but back to the story.

"Wait, you know him?" Rebecca asks.

"Yep, he is one of our neighbors on our street. Now I need to go clean up and catch up with our neighbor. So if you would, please excuse us," I say, totally forgetting that I am soaking wet and my anger at Rebecca.

I grab Brandon's hand and drag him to the back of the plane by the bathroom. "What are you doing here? Don't try to pretend you are someone else, Brandon. Also, what in the world are you doing, if you are sneaking off, exposing yourself?" I ask.

"How did you know it was me? Also, they poured ice cold water on top of you. What was I supposed to do, just let that happen to you?" Brandon replies.

"Well, thank you for standing up for me, but if you don't remember, I have had to stand Rebecca for all my life and that was one of her nicer tricks. You are also lucky that Miss Jewel was in first class," I say. "Now, if you would please excuse me, I really do have to clean myself up."

Brandon heads back to his seat, and at the same time, Haley and Blair come to help me. "Ali, I am so sorry! I should have done something about it, but that stranger seemed to have it handled. By the way, who was that?" Haley asks.

"Oh, just Brandon coming back to Oregon with us and apparently not thinking about exposing himself," I say.

Haley and Blair both have their mouths open, and they ask at the same time, "What? How did you know that?"

"Well, his voice for one and second who else would have snuck onto a plane and stick up for someone they don't know?" I ask.

At that time Emma, Olivia, and Isabelle come and say, "Oh, how could she! She is so terrible and Lily, that traitor! Also, who was that?"

"Oh, just Brandon," I say.

"What!" they exclaim.

"Yeah, just sneaking off to Oregon I guess."

"What!" they exclaim again.

"He came on the plane and is trying to hide, and he still stuck up for you. Isn't that sweet," says Isabelle.

"Yeah, I guess so. I kind of got mad at him. I should probably go apologize after I clean up," I say. I throw something on that I brought on my carry-on bag because you never know what Rebecca is going to do.

After that, I text Brandon and ask if he can meet me in the back of the plane. He texts me back and says yes. When we meet, he says, "You said you wanted to talk."

"Yeah," I say, "I just wanted to say that I'm sorry for getting mad at you and thanks for sticking up for me. I just didn't want you to get caught. You coming to Oregon with us would mean a lot to Blair," I add quickly.

"Oh," he says, sounding a little disappointed but then says happily, "Yeah, I thought she would like that."

"Thanks again. I had better get back to my seat. I have been away from it long enough, and the seat belt light just went on." I add, "Also, try and meet us outside of our tour bus. My friends and I can try and help you get a ride to our place. We can find you a place to stay later."

"Okay, I will be there," he says. "See you then."

I go back to meet my friends, all crowding around talking. "What is it?" I ask.

"Did you just tell Brandon we could give him a ride and try to find a place where he can stay?" Haley asks.

"Yeah, because that way, Blair will be able to see him whenever she wants. Also, the seat belt light just went on, so we should probably get back to our seats," I say.

Chapter 9

We get off the plane at 10:00 p.m. Since it is so late, we have a good feeling of getting Brandon somewhere in the tour bus. I say to Miss Jewel, "Miss Jewel, I am going to go to the bathroom really quickly."

"Okay," she replies.

I go to meet Brandon over by the bathrooms, and he asks, "So where do you want me to go? Also, how far is your home?"

"Oh, it isn't far. We just have the tour bus in case we have to go somewhere far away," I say. "I think that you could either hide in the bathroom or where we keep the luggage. We could probably get you in the bathroom because everyone will be too tired to use it." I say at the look on his face when I say to put him in with the luggage.

"Okay, that's fine with me," he answers.

"We had better get you into the bathroom before anyone else boards the bus. Just try to look casual when you do it. The door should be unlocked," I say.

"Okay, I'll go and do that," he says.

I go back over to the group, and my friends and I try to stall everyone so Brandon can get into the tour bus unnoticed. Emma says, "We really shouldn't rush into the tour bus. We should really admire the beautiful airport."

"The airport," says Miss Jewel, "I for one want to get home. Come on, girls."

I say to the girls, "Let's hope that Brandon is hidden well." When we get to the tour bus, we don't see any signs of Brandon, so we think we are in the clear. We start heading home, and everyone goes to sleep, except me and Haley. We are both too scared to sleep because we think that at any moment someone could discover Brandon. I say to Haley, "I am going to check if Brandon is all right."

"Okay," she replies sleepily.

I get up and go over to the bathroom and knock. I hear a voice saying, "Who is it? This bathroom is occupied," Brandon says in a terrible attempt at a girl voice.

"Brandon, it's me Ali," I say.

"Oh, okay, come in," he replies in his normal voice.

I open the door and see him standing up like he is welcoming me into his home.

I try not to laugh, but considering that this isn't his home and that it is a bathroom on our tour bus, I laugh a little. "You know what," he says, "this is actually a good bathroom, considering it is on a tour bus."

"Yeah, so I came to check if you were all right and to discuss how you are going to get off the bus without anyone knowing you were on it," I say. "Any ideas?"

"You and your friends could be the last ones on the bus and make a little circle around me. Then when we are all clear I will run away down an alleyway. Also, anywhere I could sleep tonight?" Brandon suggests.

"I like the plan," I say. "That reminds me if you keep running down that alleyway, you will come to a dead end. If you look to your left, there will be a ladder. Climb that and you will find a little tree house on a balcony. You can stay there for tonight. Tomorrow we will try to find you a better place to stay."

"Okay, sounds good," he says. "When are we going to get there?"

"In about ten minutes," I say. "I had better get back to my seat."

"Ali, I—" Brandon says.

"Yes," I reply.

"Never mind, it isn't important," he says.

"Okay, bye for now," I say back. I wonder what he wanted to tell me as I go back to my seat.

Ten minutes later, we arrive at Miss Jewel's House for Girls. I tell my friends the plan, and we stay on the bus. Since Miss Jewel is so tired, she doesn't ask us why we don't go to bed and just goes inside. We wait until everyone goes inside, then we make our move. We follow the plan exactly and it goes well.

We all say goodbye to Brandon when I remember something. "Brandon, wait. We have to decide who is going with you to find a better place to stay," I say.

Emma, Olivia, and Isabelle all say, "Well, since we are so new here and don't know our way around, I don't think that we should help."

"I have chores to do, and Blair asked me to show her around. Also, Ali, since you have gone exploring the most and know your way around, why don't you go with Brandon?" Haley asks as she smiles.

"Okay, I will go with Brandon to help him find a better place to stay," I say.

"Okay, it is a date. I mean like we will meet tomorrow which is a date," Brandon says.

"I will come up and meet you at 9:00 a.m.," I say, blushing.

We leave Brandon and go into the house.

Since we are all so tired, we decide to go to sleep but not before I say to the girls, "You all did that on purpose."

"I don't know what you are talking about," Haley says.

"Have fun tomorrow," Emma says.

"Good night, guys," I say, still blushing. I think, *What am I going to do?*

Chapter 10

The next morning, I start to do the chores. Eventually, I realize I am going to be late meeting Brandon, so I ask Haley, "Hey, can you cover for me while I am showing Brandon around?"

"Sure, have fun and tell us everything when you get back," she replies.

"Okay, see you," I say. I start heading back down the alleyway to our little clubhouse.

When I climb the ladder, I am surprised to see that the clubhouse is cleaned up, considering we haven't been in it for at least a year. "Brandon," I say, "are you ready to go look around the town?"

He pops up from behind a small chair and says, "Yep, where are we going first, and do you have suggestions on where I could stay? Not saying that this place isn't great, it can just get a little cold sometimes."

"I was thinking about somewhere near the park. It is not too far away, but there is a place that one of our friends lives; and she is out of town right now, so her place is free. She also said we could use it if we needed to," I reply.

"Sounds good to me. After that, can you show me around your town?" Brandon asks.

"Yeah, sure. If you would just follow me," I say as I lead him over on a different path.

We start walking to the park, and I look over at Brandon and see his features more closely. He has brown hair and blue eyes; and the more I look at him, the more I think he is cute. I have the urge to tell him I like him, but I still feel like it is too early.

Brandon asks, "So what is your favorite color?"

I answer, "Mine is blue. What about yours?"

"I like green," he replies.

"How long have you been at your orphanage?" I ask him.

"For as long as I can remember. What about you?" he asks.

"Same here. Oh, and would you look at that. Here is one place that I thought had all the necessities you would need," I say.

We go into the house, and Brandon says, "Well, looks good to me. Where are you going to take me now?"

"I was thinking that we could rent some bikes, and we could ride around town. I could show you everything," I say.

"Oh yeah, that sounds fun," he replies.

We get on our bikes, and I start showing him around the town; and eventually, we get to my favorite spot, a huge weeping willow tree that I haven't shown anyone except Haley. "Wow," Brandon gasps. "This is such a pretty spot."

"Yeah, this is where I go to feel happy or to get away from Rebecca. I call it the secret place," I reply.

"She must be really mean to you. She has been there as long as you too. Trust me, I didn't trust her as soon as I saw her," Brandon says.

"Yeah, I don't know why she never liked me and Haley because we have never done anything to her," I say. "Want to go underneath the branches? It is even more magical on the inside."

"Sure," he replies.

We go to the center of the weeping willow. We talk for a while about what has happened since we have been in our orphanages and about our families too.

I look at my clock and realize that it is 5:00 p.m. How have we been together for that long? "Brandon, I am so sorry, but I have to go. Miss Jewel and everyone else is going to wonder where I am. I am so sorry. Probably see you tonight if Blair will want to see you," I say.

"Okay. Bye. Text me if you come," he replies.

I rush back to the house and get there just as Miss Jewel calls, "Girls, time for dinner." I rush to get washed up then go to the table and once again sit on the floor. My friends and I all eat quickly because they all want to hear the details of my outing.

After dinner, we head upstairs, and I get bombarded with questions. Haley bursts out, "How was your date? What did you do?"

I answer, "Guys, first of all, it was not a date. It was an outing. Second of all, we really just talked."

"Where did you go?" Olivia asks.

"The weeping willow," I answer quietly because I know what's coming.

"You took him to the weeping willow. The one you have only ever shown me," says Haley.

"Yes," I answer.

"Romantic place, check. By yourselves, check. Talk the whole time, check. Yep, that is all the checks for a date," says Isabelle.

"Girls, it's your turn to do the dishes," Miss Jewel calls up.

"Be down in a minute," Emma answers.

"Just one more question." Blair asks, "Are you and my brother ever going to tell each other that you like each other?"

"I don't know, Blair. I will think about it," I answer.

We go downstairs to do the dishes when Rebecca comes out and says, "Oh, is the little baby still here? Where's her binky and shouldn't she be taking her little nap?"

Blair starts crying and runs upstairs. Haley goes up the stairs, running after her, but before I go up too, I ask Rebecca, "Why do you have to be so mean? What did she ever do to you?"

Olivia calls after me, "We will do the dishes. You just stay up there."

"Thanks," I call back.

I go into our bedroom and see Blair is still crying. I ask her, "Blair, are you okay?"

"Yeah, just why did she do that? What did I ever do to her?"

"I asked the same thing," I say.

After about twenty minutes, Emma, Olivia, and Isabelle come back up. I ask Haley, Emma, Olivia, and Isabelle, "Hey, can I talk to you guys alone?"

"Sure," they answer.

We go out of earshot of Blair then I say, "Girls, I think that Blair needs to be Rebecca free for a little while, and she probably needs to have someone go with her. By that I mean two people should go with Blair for two days and stay with her brother. So whoever goes will not be here for two days."

"I agree," says Haley. "But who should go with her?"

"I think that Ali and Haley should go with her because they are the ones that she trusts the most, and she has been saying you two are like her sisters," says Emma.

"I agree and you should probably leave tonight. Don't worry, we will cover for you," says Isabelle.

"Okay, we will do that, but first let me text Brandon."

I grab my phone and text Brandon that Haley, Blair, and I are coming over, and we are staying there for a few days, and I will explain when we get there. I tell Blair and she seems excited. We each get a backpack of stuff ready, and at 10:00 p.m., we leave.

We say goodbye to Emma, Olivia, and Isabelle and head toward the park. When we get to the place where Brandon is staying, I knock on the door and hear his voice saying, "Come in." Blair runs over and hugs him, which is really cute.

Brandon tells Blair, "Okay, I am going to go talk to Ali for a minute, but I will be right back." Haley goes off to talk to Blair while Brandon comes over to talk to me.

I start telling him the story and tell him what we are going to do over the next few days. He agrees with the plan, and we go back over to Haley and Blair. I say,

"It's getting kind of late, so I think we should all get some rest. Good night."

"Good night," they all say back.

I try to go to sleep, but I can't stop thinking about why Rebecca said what she said to Blair. Again, like it has been the last few nights, I am about to drift off to sleep when I hear footsteps and see silhouettes. I see them put something to Haley and Blair's face, and I am thinking it is some sort of sleeping draught. Then they take Blair and Haley and put them in bags. The next thing I know, it is pitch-black.

Chapter 11

Next thing I know, I am tied up in a little log cabin. It is cold considering it is summer. I realize that Haley, Blair, and Brandon are also tied up, but they are still knocked out. I look around and try to see a way to get out of here, but first of all, I should probably figure out where we are. Fortunately, there is a map on the table of Michigan. Michigan! I think I must have been knocked out for a long time considering that we came from Oregon to Michigan.

I hear that Brandon is waking, and I say, "Brandon, we got captured and now we're in Michigan."

"Michigan, how in the world did we get to Michigan?" he asks.

I tell him, "I wasn't fully asleep when these guys came in. They put something to our mouths, so I am guessing that it was a sleeping draught. It knocked us out and here we are." By this time, Haley and Blair are awake and hear my story too.

We hear footsteps coming our way, so we all go quiet. I heard this deep voice and see this man who has a big mustache and beard, and he is saying, "Don't worry, no one will find them." Then he turns around and sees that we are awake and says, "Well, well, well, look who's up."

"Who are you and why did you bring us here?" I demand.

"We didn't mean to take you two girls," he says, pointing at me and Haley. "But we weren't sure which of you was which, so we just took you all."

"What can we have that interests you?" Brandon asks, sounding puzzled. "We are orphans. We don't have anything special."

"Oh, that's where you're wrong," says the man. "But first let's make proper introductions. My name is Samuel and you are?" he asks me.

"I am Ali, also an orphan, but why do you want to know?" I question.

"Just seeing as you will be here for a long time, we should know each other's names," he replies, obviously getting annoyed.

"My name is Haley. What do you mean we are staying here for a long time?" Haley questions.

"If we finish the introductions, I will tell you the story," says the man named Samuel.

"Okay then, I am Blair," says Blair.

"And I am Brandon, but I still don't understand why you want me and my sister," Brandon says.

"Okay, seeing that we finished the introductions, I should probably tell you the story now," says Samuel. "It all started when you two went to that orphanage. You see you went to that orphanage, not because your parents didn't love you, it is because they were just trying to keep you safe from us."

"What are you talking about?" Brandon asks.

"If you let me finish, I can tell you," Samuel replies. "Have you ever wondered why your parents gave the orphanage a lot of money to take care of you. Well, they are kind of rich."

"But why would they want to keep us safe?" questions Blair.

Samuel replies, "It is because they are investing in a secret organization called the SSOA which means Secret Spies of America. Well, long story short, we are trying to get your parents to give us money. So we decided to take their kids, and we are now asking them for money to get you two back."

"What about us? What are you going to do with us?" Haley and I ask at the same time.

"We were thinking you are their friends, right? Now we can get even more money for you two and your friends," replies Samuel.

"Who is the boss?" Brandon demands. "Because obviously you aren't considering you just told us your whole plan. That move is never smart."

"I will give you a hint. You all have met him before," Samuel says, being a little annoyed at being told what he did wrong by a thirteen-year-old. "Sit tight. We will be splitting you up tomorrow. So you won't know what happens to the other two. Since Brandon and Blair are brother and sister, we should probably — "

"Have us stay together," Blair interrupts.

"What? No way, and since you like Ali a little more than Haley, you will stay with Haley in one room, and Brandon and Ali will stay in the other."

"Are you going to keep us tied up while we are here, or are you going to just lock us in a room with no way to escape?" I question.

"The boss doesn't want anything bad to happen to all of you because if we hand you over unharmed, maybe we can get more money," Samuel replies.

Chapter 12

The next morning, true to his word, we are split up into two rooms. I am with Brandon and Haley is with Blair. That morning, Samuel says, "We don't have any Wi-Fi so don't try and get in touch with anyone."

"That's just great, and it's all my fault for getting Blair captured. If we would have just stayed there, we probably wouldn't have been captured. They probably followed us around and figured out where you were staying. This is all my fault," I say when I am locked up in the room with Brandon.

I don't want to break down in front of Blair, and at the same time, I know Brandon wouldn't judge me. Even though we have kind of just met, it feels like we have been friends forever. "Ali, settle down. First of all, it is not your fault, and second of all, if you should blame anyone, it should be me or Rebecca. I bet that they saw me jump on your bus and saw that it was me and realized my sister was there too. Or you should blame Rebecca because if she hadn't said what she said, you wouldn't have had the idea to run away and come find me," Brandon replies.

"I know," I say. "But I still feel like you should all be mad at me."

"Be mad at you? Why would we be mad at you? Every one of us is probably thinking that it is their fault and saying the same thing. At least you saw what was happening while the rest of us were just sleeping," Brandon says. "Right now, we need to think of a way to get out of here."

"Oh no," I say. "I just remembered Emma, Olivia, and Isabelle think that we won't be back for two days, and since we don't have any Wi-Fi, we won't be able to tell them that we need help." But at that same time, I hear a ding which sort of sounds like my phone getting a text. I look at it and see that Haley has just texted me, "Okay, so looks like we do have Wi-Fi. Samuel just said that because he didn't want us to text anyone. I found out because Samuel was walking us to our room. I saw a bunch of computers, and they can't use them without Wi-Fi."

I reply, "Okay, I will text Olivia. Thank you so much!" I tell Brandon and text Olivia, "Help," and I am about to text more, but the Wi-Fi goes all wacky so I can't send more.

Then we hear Samuel's voice over the speaker that I didn't even know was in the room. He says, "Good job figuring out that we have Wi-Fi, but now we have cut off all communication to the outside world, so good luck trying to get help now."

"Oh no, I only had time to text 'help' and send it before communication was cut off. They could think that means anything." I text Haley, "They could think I need help telling Brandon that I like him."

It is about dinner time, and we don't even get fresh meals. At least we have a tiny mini fridge that has a supply of food in it that will last a little while. Brandon and I start brainstorming ideas to get out of this place, and so far, we don't have anything good.

During dinner, we barely talk, but Brandon says after a little bit of silence, "Maybe the SSOA will come save us."

"Yeah, maybe but that probably won't be for a week or two considering it will probably take the girls another day to realize that we really need help. Then they would have to locate us and figure out a plan to get us without paying a lot of money," I say.

By this time, it is around 9:00 p.m., so I say, "Sorry for being so negative, but I still feel like it is all my fault, and we should probably get to bed. We will need our strength if we are going to last another day in this place. I actually look around the room that we have been put in and realize that there is only one bed, so I say, "You should have the bed because they want to make you comfortable," I say. "Besides I deserve to sleep on the floor," I add quietly to myself.

"No, you should have the bed. You haven't had as much sleep. Also, you don't deserve to sleep on the floor," Brandon replies.

So he did hear that. "Thanks," I tell him. "Good night."

"Good night," he says back. After I am sure that Brandon is asleep, I just start thinking about everything. Then I think of Blair being separated from her brother and I don't mean to, but I start crying. I hear that Brandon is waking up, and I try to stop myself.

Brandon says, "Ali, are you okay?"

I try to say yes but I can't, so I say, "No, I am so sorry that you and your sister are separated, and it is all my fault. She needs you and I got you separated."

Brandon goes to turn on the light and comes to sit on the bed with me and says, "Ali, it isn't your fault. If anything, you helped us. You didn't turn me in while we were in the plane, and you found me a place to stay so I can still see Blair."

"But now you can't, and we are in this terrible place. I am so sorry," I say.

"Ali, if anyone needs to be sorry it is me because I got you into this mess. They wouldn't have brought you and Haley here if you weren't with us, and it is my fault. Please don't cry," he replies.

I grab a Kleenex and try to stop crying. I put my head on Brandon's shoulder and say, "Your sister has become like a sister to me, and I don't want her to be hurt or sad."

"Ali, you are like a sister to her too, and I want to thank you for taking such good care of her," Brandon says.

"I am so sorry for waking you up and really sorry that you have to help me. I just can't bear to see Blair sad, and now you can't even be with her," I say.

"Ali, it is okay. Why don't we try to get some sleep so we can try to find a way out of here tomorrow," Brandon says.

"Okay, sorry again," I reply. As soon as my head hits the pillow, I fall asleep.

Chapter 13

The next morning, I wake up at nine o'clock, and Brandon and I don't really talk. I am thinking that he thinks I am weird because I cried, but I hope we can still be friends. "Ali, I would just like to tell you that I think it is very sweet that you cried because you didn't want Blair to be sad," says Brandon. "Not many people care about others, like Rebecca for instance."

"Oh, thanks. I guess she really does feel like a sister to me," I reply.

I guess he doesn't think it is crazy that I cried. That makes me like him even more. "So, what should we do today?" he asks.

"I think that I should text Haley. We can see if they have ideas to get out of here. Then we could do some brainstorming," I say.

"That sounds good," he replies.

So I text Haley, "Hey, do you guys have any ideas about how to get out of this place?"

"No, do you guys yet and you have your charger, right? So we can still text because that is the only way we can still communicate," Haley asks.

"Yes, luckily, I had my phone bag on me when they kidnapped us. What about you?" I reply.

"Same here, well got to go," she texts.

"One more question, how is Blair doing?" I text.

"She is doing fine, but she misses you guys. How are you doing?" she texts back.

"Okay, I mean I kind of started crying when I thought of Blair without her brother, but Brandon comforted me, and he doesn't think I am weird because I did it. He actually thinks it is sweet," I text.

"Well, that's good. So are you going to tell him?" she asks.

"Maybe, I have been thinking about it, but I am not sure yet," I reply.

"Well, I have to go. Keep brainstorming."

I start thinking of ways to get out of here and a little about if I should tell Brandon that I like him. I think maybe I should because even Blair said that he liked me. So I think that I will tell him a little later. Maybe, it just depends. "Thought of anything yet?" I ask Brandon.

"Not except to wait until either my parents pay for us or the SSOA comes and gets us. What about you, and how are they doing?" Brandon asks.

"I haven't had a breakthrough yet. They are doing fine, and your sister is holding up, but she misses us," I say.

"We miss her too," he says.

"Why don't we take a break and think about something totally unrelated to our situation now? We need a break." I suggest.

"Okay, what is your favorite subject in school?" he asks me.

"I like history. What about you?" I ask.

"I like history too, but I also like math," he answers.

I start singing because it is what I do when I don't know what to do.

"Wow, you have an amazing voice!" Brandon says.

"Oh, thanks. I guess I just learned," I say.

"What song was that? I don't think I have heard it," he says.

"Well, I kind of wrote it," I reply.

"You wrote that!" Brandon exclaims.

"Yeah," I say.

"Here, teach me. I know how to sing too," he says.

"You do?" I ask, totally blown away.

"Yeah, I used to sing Blair to sleep," he says.

"Okay, well it goes like this. 'You may be scared sometimes and not know what to do. You might not know what to do sometimes but who do you look to. There are so many people in this world who can help you. Just ask, ask, ask for help. Ask, ask, ask for help, and you will find it and you will find it.'" I sing.

"That's good. Now let's sing it together," he says. We start singing and eventually realize that it is time for dinner.

"That was really fun. Thanks for that," I say.

"Hey, you're the one with the great songs," he replies. We sit in silence, but then I decide what I have been struggling to do from this morning.

At the same time, Brandon and I say, "I need to tell you something."

"You can go first," I say.

"Ali, I have been wanting to tell you this from the time you bumped into me. Ali, I like you," he says.

I stare at him then I remember I was going to say something, too, so I say, "Brandon, I have also wanted to tell you this from the time I met you. I like you too."

Chapter 14

We sit, staring at each other for at least five minutes. I am just speechless and don't know what to say. I think Brandon is feeling the same way. I decide to get my phone and text Haley. "Haley, I did it! I told Brandon and he feels the same way. What should I say?"

"Girl! Good job. Just ask if he wants some dinner now," Haley replies.

I take Haley's advice and say to Brandon, "Want some dinner?"

"Sure," Brandon replies.

While I am going to get dinner ready, Brandon and I hear Haley and Blair jumping up and down yelling, "Yes, yes, yes! They did it! They did it!"

Brandon and I look at each other and just start laughing. "So you have liked me since we met," Brandon asks.

"Yeah, and same with you?" I ask.

He says, "Yep, and your friends and my sister told me to tell you, but I thought—"

"That it was too early, and it would be weird," I continue.

"Then my sister," Brandon says, "told me you liked me and said just do it."

"So we pretty much had the same thing happen," I say.

"Yep, that's pretty much what happened," Brandon replies.

After dinner, we decide we should go to sleep, but I ask, "Brandon, do you think that we will ever escape because tomorrow would be the third day which means that Emma, Olivia, and Isabelle will start to worry."

"I think that we will get out of here, but right now let's not worry about that because being stuck here means I am with you," he replies. I blush and personally being stuck with Brandon doesn't sound too bad. The next morning, Brandon and I talk more about how we might escape.

During breakfast, I tell him how my friends had me go alone with him to find a place to stay which neither of us were too mad about. I decide to look at the news to see if there are any reports on missing children, and I find one. "Brandon, look at this. It went up online at five this morning. It says that four orphans have gone missing, and it has our pictures. Sources have said that these four ran away and were supposed to be back in two days, but one of the girls texted 'Help.' Their friends thought it was about something else, but it looks as if they really do need help," I say.

At that moment, Samuel's voice came over the speaker saying, "You must have seen the notice that four kids are missing, but they won't find you here. Also, Brandon and Ali you guys are really cute together, good job for telling each other."

"Was he just telling us we did a good job of telling each other that we like each other?" Brandon asks.

"I think so," I reply. "I hope the SSOA can find us or someone can because I really don't want your parents to pay money to get me and Haley out of this place."

"I hope the SSOA can find us, but I will make our parents, that I don't even know, pay money for you and Haley because you are our best friends. We will not let you stay here if they don't pay," Brandon says.

"Thanks, but you really shouldn't. I just want you and Blair to be safe," I reply.

"Well, I want you and Haley to be safe," Brandon says back. "So you will get out of here with us too, okay?"

"Okay, I just hope they get here soon," I reply.

We spend another day trying to figure out how to get out of here. At the end of day, we are about to go back to sleep when we hear a helicopter. "Do you hear that?" I ask Brandon.

"Yeah, I do," he replies.

CHAPTER 14

Then we hear an unknown voice saying, "Give up and come out with your hands raised."

"The SSOA, they found us!" I exclaim.

Chapter 15

"No way, that was fast!" Brandon says.

"I am Officer Robinson, president of the SSOA. Kids, don't worry. We will get you out of there," says Officer Robinson.

"We are going home. We are going home. Wow, I didn't think that I would ever find a place I liked less than Miss Jewel's, but this definitely wins," I say.

The next minute, the door is open, and we are finally let out of that room. Brandon and Blair hug each other and so do me and Haley. "Thank you so much," I tell Officer Robinson.

"No, don't thank us. We are just doing our job. Now, do you guys know who is running this operation," Officer Robinson asks.

"Well, considering the tip that Samuel gave us," Blair says.

"We think that it is—" Haley says.

"Mr. Stephens," Brandon and I say at the same time.

"How did you guys figure that out?" asks Samuel. "I thought you would think that it is someone totally different."

"So you are confirming that it is Mr. Stephens," asks a woman I don't know. "I am Officer Robinson of the SSOA."

"Oh no, the boss is going to kill me!" says Samuel.

"Not where you're going. You will be under constant watch and so will Mr. Stephens. He is still in the house I presume," says Officer Robinson, the woman.

"I will go check around the house," says a man whose badge says Smith.

"Thanks, Smith," says Officer Robinson, the man. "You're coming with us."

After all the arrest and catching Mr. Stephens, who tried to run away, my friends and I get in a helicopter with both of the Officer Robinsons while the captives get in another. When we start flying, what I am assuming is back home. Officer Robinson, the man, says, "Hello, I know it might be hard for us to tell which Officer Robinson you are talking to so you can call me Mr. Robinson or Zack, and you can call my wife Mrs. Robinson or Amy."

"Hi," I say, assuming we should introduce ourselves too. "I am Ali and thank you for saving us from them."

"My name is Haley. I would also like to thank you for saving us from them," says Haley.

"I am Brandon," says Brandon. "Thank you, but why were those guys trying to capture us?"

"I am Blair," says Blair. "And are our parents really investing in the SSOA?"

Mr. and Mrs. Robinson sit, staring at us then at each other, but then Mrs. Robinson pulls herself together and says, "Those guys are called Rebels, who do not like the government, and are trying to take over America. The reason they wanted to take you is because your parents have a lot of money."

Mr. Robinson apparently finding his voice too says, "Yes, it is true that your parents invest in the SSOA, and they are actually good friends of ours. Also, just to let you know we are the presidents of the SSOA."

"Cool," I say. "But how did you find us so fast?"

"Well, luckily for us, your friends that you texted 'Help' too helped us find the tracking devices that you all have on your phones. Thanks to you guys for being prepared and having your chargers so we were able to see your location," replies Mrs. Robinson.

"Now we want to ask you some questions," Mr. Robinson says, turning to Brandon and Blair. "Did you know that Mr. Stephens was bad?"

"No, we had no idea. I mean we didn't like him, but we didn't think he was bad," replies Brandon.

"What exactly happened the night you were taken?" asks Mrs. Robinson.

"That would be a question for Ali," replies Blair.

"Well," I say, "I was trying to go to sleep when I heard these footsteps coming in through the door. I looked and saw two silhouettes of men. They drugged Haley and Blair with what I think was a sleeping draught. The next thing I know everything went black, and when I woke up, we were in Michigan."

"That is great information, young lady. I think that is it. We will be taking you back to Miss Jewel's House for Girls now," says Mr. Robinson.

Chapter 16

When we get back to Miss Jewel's House for Girls, we thank Mr. and Mrs. Robinson again and say goodbye. We go into the house, and as soon as we get inside, we are bombarded with hugs and questions mostly from Emma, Olivia, and Isabelle. Miss Jewel is there too, and she yells, "Girls, how dare you run away and then get yourselves captured! Have I not taught you better?"

"Now wait just one second," says Brandon. "If you haven't noticed the reason, they were coming to see me and run away for a few days because of Rebecca and what she said to my sister. So maybe you should ask her some more questions."

"Oh, well, I am sorry, but I don't think that you have the authority to tell me what to do, now do you," replies Miss Jewel.

"I can't believe you. We have done nothing but put up with you always praising Rebecca and giving us all of the chores, telling us off for things that we didn't do, and you have never told Rebecca off for everything she does to us," I say, getting angry.

"And what has Rebecca been doing? Is she insulting you too? Is it hurting your feelings?" asks Miss Jewel.

"If you haven't realized by now, Rebecca has been throwing water all over Ali really early in the morning. Oh, and remember when you thought we pushed her when we first came here, well she pushed Ali and she ended up spraining her ankle. Rebecca got off but Ali and I had to do all the work," says Haley.

"Okay, but do you have any proof of this?" Miss Jewel asks.

"Did you have any proof when you accused me and Haley of everything Rebecca did?" I ask.

"Well no—" starts Miss Jewel.

"If you would please excuse us, we have had a long couple of days. You know being kidnapped and all, so we would like to go to our bedroom and rest," says Blair. Miss Jewel just stares at all of us when we head upstairs followed by Emma, Olivia, and Isabelle who are also staring at us.

When we get upstairs, Emma says, "I can't believe you guys did that."

"I mean standing up to Miss Jewel," says Olivia.

"That could have gotten you into even more trouble, but you were brave enough to tell her the truth," says Isabelle.

"We have been wanting to say that forever," I say.

"Thanks for helping us," I add to Brandon.

He replies, "No problem. Just thought I could help."

"Well, anyway." Isabelle says after the awkward moment. "What happened?"

"You know what, I think I am going to head out. I am really tired after being kidnapped. See you later," Brandon says.

"Wait, Brandon, I think that Miss Jewel will let you stay in the finished attic. It might not be the best place, but it would be better to be closer to Blair, right?" I ask.

"Yeah, thanks, Ali," Brandon replies.

After Brandon leaves, Emma says, "So we still want to know what happened. Start from the very beginning."

"Okay, okay, okay, I will tell you. Well, it all started with me about to go to sleep and then we were drugged and kidnapped. I woke up, and luckily, there was a map that said we were in Michigan. After that, we discovered why they kidnapped us. Samuel, a bad guy, came and explained it all. They did it because they thought they would get money from Brandon and Blair's parents to get their children back. Well, we were split up into rooms, Brandon and I in one room and Haley and Blair in the other. We kept brainstorming ways to get out, but we never figured that out. When Brandon and I were together, I started singing a song I wrote. Then I taught it to Brandon, and we sang it together," I say.

"Wait one second. You and Brandon sang together! You never told me that!" exclaims Haley.

"Sorry, I forgot," I reply. "Anyways, after that Brandon and I sort of told each other that we like each other."

"You guys told each other!" Emma, Olivia, and Isabelle exclaim.

"Yeah," I reply. "We went to sleep and saw that a notice went up with four kids missing. Then the SSOA came and now we are here."

"You told him," Olivia still looks stunned as she says it.

"Yeah," I reply.

Then something I thought would happen, happened. All of the girls got up and started jumping saying, "She told him! She told him! She told him!"

"Oh, look who's back," says a voice I would be happy not to have heard at that time.

"Oh, hi, Rebecca," I say. "Miss us?"

"Not one bit, but I did miss pouring water on someone," Rebecca replies.

"So what did Ali tell who?"

"Ali told Brandon she likes him!" exclaims Isabelle.

"Oh," says Rebecca. "Then you must be really sad because he turned you down, didn't he?"

"For your information, he actually said he likes her too. Also, he told me he would rather go out with anyone but you," replies Blair.

"Oh, okay. Well if you would please excuse me," says Rebecca, and she storms off and I can still hear her crying by the time she gets down the hall.

"Hey, guys," I hear a voice I also wouldn't want to hear at this time. "What's up?"

"Oh, nothing much just got back from being kidnapped," I say. "What about you, Lily?"

"Oh, nothing much," replies Lily.

"Sorry, Lily, but I am actually really tired you know. Being kidnapped can be really tiring. So, bye," I say.

Then Lily goes off the way Rebecca went.

"Actually, guys, I am really tired, so I am going to go to sleep. Good night," I say.

Chapter 17

The next morning, it was back to chores again. Apparently, being kidnapped doesn't count for anything here. At 10:00 a.m., there was a knock on the door, and I say, "I will get it." I open the door and standing there are no doubt Blair and Brandon's parents.

"Hello, I assume you are here to see Brandon and Blair," I say.

"Yes," they reply.

"Why don't you come in and have a seat, and I will get them for you," I say.

"That would be lovely," Brandon's mom says.

"I will be right back. Please make yourselves at home," I reply.

I leave Brandon and Blair's parents to go find Brandon and Blair. I find them doing some chores in the kitchen. As soon as I find them, I say, "Guys, your parents are here."

"What?" they reply.

"Your parents are here," I repeat. "They are waiting in the sitting room. I will take you to them."

On the way back to the sitting room, we meet Haley; and I tell her what is happening and say, "They might want to see us too seeing as we were with them when they were kidnapped."

We get back down to the sitting room, and when Brandon and Blair see their parents, they don't go running up to them. They just stare at them and funnily enough so do the parents. To break the silence, I say, "Hello, my name is Ali."

Haley following along says, "Hi, my name is Haley."

After we say that, it seems to break the tension in the room. Brandon's dad says, "Hello, my name is Mike, and this is my wife Taylor. You could also call us Mr. and Mrs. Williams."

"I am Brandon, and this is Blair," says Brandon.

After that little introduction, what I was expecting since we entered this room happened.

"Why did you leave us? Why did you never reach out to us? Do you know how hard it is to be orphans, and all the adults show you favoritism because their parents have a lot of money? Or be questioned why your parents left you even though they are still alive and have enough money to care for you?" asks Brandon, angrily.

"Brandon, it is okay. Why don't you let them explain?" I ask.

"Okay? Okay? How can you say it is okay when you don't know if your parents are dead or not? You haven't had to deal with people asking you that question," he shouts back at me.

"You're right. I don't know if my parents are alive or not, but at least you have parents who are alive and who did that to protect you. I don't know what happened to my parents and even if they are still alive or not, but you should be thankful you have parents who are alive. You have Blair to look after, I know, but she keeps you company and you have a sibling to share the pain with, and I don't. I don't know why you are complaining about being bullied because if you haven't realized, I have been bullied my whole life by Rebecca. I also just lost one of my best friends because she was sick of having to do all the chores and not being Miss Jewel's favorite. So, yes, I am so sorry for you, but if you haven't realized, we have had it hard too," I shout back before I storm upstairs.

A few minutes later, Haley comes up and says, "Ali, I am so sorry that happened."

"Don't be. If that's how he feels, then let him be angry at his parents who still love him and are still alive. We both don't know where our parents are or if they are even alive," I reply.

A minute later, Mrs. Williams comes in and says, "I am so sorry for my son's behavior."

"Thank you for apologizing, but you don't need to. It is Brandon who needs to apologize," I reply.

A few minutes later, Mrs. Williams says, "So I hear that you two were also kidnapped by the Rebels."

"Yes," Haley replies.

"I am sorry it happened, but at least we caught who was behind it all," Mrs. Williams replies.

"I don't know about that," I say. "I mean, yes, Mr. Stephens was behind capturing us, but that was just to get money. I think someone else is the leader of the Rebels."

"Maybe we should go back downstairs so we can talk more about what happened," Mrs. Williams suggests.

"Yes, that's fine," I say.

When we go back downstairs, I do my best not to look at Brandon. Mr. Williams says, "Well, since we are all back together, could we ask about you being kidnapped?"

"Sure," I say. "What do you want to know?"

Mr. and Mrs. Williams ask a variety of questions, and we tell them everything we can. After we had finished recounting our story about being kidnapped, Mr. Williams says, "Thank you for telling us. This will really help the SSOA."

"No problem," Haley says.

"We hope we can see you again. Nice to meet you all," Mrs. Williams says.

"Nice to meet you too. Bye," I say as I slip out of the room. I rush back upstairs and see Emma, Olivia, and Isabelle sitting there ready to hear what just happened. I tell them everything, and they stare at me with their mouths open.

Then Isabelle asks, "Do you still like him?"

I say, "I am not sure."

I hear someone coming up the stairs, and sure enough Rebecca says, "Does this mean that Brandon is fair game because I think he might like me."

"Why don't you go ask him," I say.

When I hear Rebecca running down the hall, crying, I think I know what Brandon said.

"Well, I am going to sleep. Good night," I say to everyone.

Chapter 18

The next morning, I try to avoid Brandon as much as I can. I realize that I could have been a bit more understanding, but I was trying to help him. So I think that he should apologize. We are back to the chores again, and luckily, I can avoid Brandon because we don't have the same chores. Around lunch time, Blair comes and gets me and says, "Ali, we have more visitors."

"Great," I say unenthusiastically. "Who is it now?"

"Mr. and Mrs. Robinson," she replies.

"Be there in a minute," I say.

I finish the dishes and head to the sitting room. When I walk into the sitting room, everyone is already there. "Hi, Ali. How are you doing?" Mrs. Robinson asks.

"Good. What about you?" I say.

"We are doing fine. Thanks for asking," Mrs. Robinson replies.

"Well, let's get down to business. You probably know why we are here, but I will tell you," says Mr.

Robinson. "We would like to get some of your views on the Rebels and why you got kidnapped."

"I think that they just wanted to capture Blair and Brandon," I say, "because they wanted to get money from Mr. and Mrs. Williams."

"Yes, that makes sense, but do you think that Mr. Stephens and Samuel are the heads of the Rebels," asks Mr. Robinson.

"I personally don't think so. First of all, I think they just wanted to make some money. Second of all, why would the leader or leaders of the Rebels tell us their whole plan?" I ask.

"Good point. Do you think that Samuel and Mr. Stephens thought that you girls were special?" asks Mrs. Robinson.

"No, I mean we don't even know about our parents, so I doubt they thought that Ali and I were special," says Haley.

"Yeah, I agree. I mean Samuel even said that maybe they could get some extra money from my parents because they were friends with us," says Brandon.

"That makes sense. Do you think that Mr. and Mrs. Williams would have paid money for them?" Mr. Robinson asks.

"If they didn't," says Brandon, "I would have made them. I mean they are our friends."

"If that did happen, you and your sister should have just gone. Haley and I would have found a way out on our own, besides Samuel probably would have just thrown us out, and we would just walk back to Miss Jewel's or we could get a ride," I say. I know that, that is a very nice thing for him to do, but right now I don't know if I would have appreciated it as much.

"What? So you were just going to walk all the way from Michigan to Oregon," replies Brandon.

"Well, yeah, if we had to, I would have tried, but I would be grateful if someone would offer us a ride," I say.

"Who's really going to pick up two thirteen-year-old girls? They would probably think that you were running away," Brandon replies.

"They might have, but I don't care. I would have tried to get back here because it is the only home I know. I would have done anything to get back and make sure everyone was okay, even Rebecca. Just because we aren't friends doesn't mean I don't want to know what happened to her. I would also want to make sure Blair was okay because she is like a little sister to me. So, yes, I would have walked all the way back here even if it was the last thing I did. I don't care if it would have taken me a year or the rest of my life. I would want to come back here," I say.

Brandon just stares at me. I say, "I don't know what you would have done, but that would have been my plan."

"Okay, well thank you for that information, but I would like to know how you were split up. So I can see what the Rebels would do to us if we ever got captured by them," Mr. Robinson says.

I can tell that he is trying to change the subject, and I personally don't care. Blair decides to say, "It was Haley and I and Brandon and Ali. They said that they wanted to make us sad not being with the people we know best because they thought we might become weaker."

"Sorry, but I have chores I need to get to so would you please excuse me," I say.

"You know what I need to get out of this room too. Maybe you could show me around," Mrs. Robinson says.

"Yeah, sure follow me," I say.

I show Mrs. Robinson around a little then I show her to our room, and she says, "Ali, do you mind if we talk for a minute."

"Yeah, sure," I reply. I have no idea what this could be about.

"Ali, I see that you and Brandon don't get along very well. Was it hard for you while you were locked up together?" Mrs. Robinson asks.

"Actually, no, we were good friends, but we had a fight yesterday, and I guess we are just not as good of friends as we thought we were," I reply.

"I see, I see, so does that mean that you two liked each other, but you had a fight and you probably both think that the other should apologize," Mrs. Robinson says.

"Well, yeah, but I am not sure what he feels like. Right now, I don't really know how I feel about him," I reply.

"Well, I have to go now, but maybe you could save your friendship because you both might be right and wrong in this situation. Bye," Mrs. Robinson says.

"Bye," I say, totally awestruck. Maybe she is right, but right now I don't want to go up to Brandon and say something like that. After a while, Emma, Olivia, Isabelle, Haley, and Blair come upstairs. Haley tells everyone what happened; and right about now, I don't think I want to deal with all their questions, so about halfway through Haley's retelling, I say, "I am going to go out for a bit. Don't wait up for me."

I leave the room before any of them can say anything back. I get out of the door, and I just run to where I know I can have some peace and quiet. I get to the weeping willow and go through the branches.

I think about everything that has happened since we went to London, about Brandon and Blair, about getting kidnapped, and about what Mrs. Robinson said. I see that it is getting late, but I don't go back. I am getting tired and I know I need to go back, but I am just so tired from all of this thinking that I fall asleep.

Chapter 19

I wake up and see that I am underneath the weeping willow. Oh no, I never went back to Miss Jewel's. Wait, why am I covered with a blanket? Last thing I remember, I fell asleep and I didn't have a blanket. I bet it was Haley. She would probably have been worried about me. She probably checked the weeping willow and saw I was asleep so covered me up with this blanket. *Yeah, that's probably what happened,* I think to myself.

Right now, I have to get back to Miss Jewel's or I will be in big trouble. I run back to Miss Jewel's and realize I get there just in time for breakfast. When I step into the house, I remember why I ran away for the night. I was thinking about a lot of things including Brandon. I still don't want to say that I am wrong considering that we both were right and wrong. So I do my best to ignore him.

This week, Rebecca hasn't really been mean, but I know it is coming and it isn't going to be good. I sit down on the floor again with Haley and say, "Hi, did I miss anything?"

"Nope, not much, just Rebecca being her usual self and because you weren't there, she poured water all over me," Haley replies.

"She did? Haley, I am so sorry. That should have been me," I say.

"No, trust me. It is fine, but I have no idea how you deal with that pretty much every morning," she responds.

"I guess you get used to Rebecca. I mean pouring water on people, she does that so much. I think she must have lost her nerve," I say.

"Girl, have you lost your mind," she replies.

"No, it is just I guess I am in a good mood. You wouldn't believe what sleeping under a tree can do for you," I say.

Haley laughs, but at that moment, Rebecca comes in with her gang and says, "What's so funny? Is it that you want some happiness with all of your chores, or are you trying to channel your disappointment into something happy because Brandon and I are a thing now?"

"What!" Haley and I both exclaim. I mean no one would expect that Rebecca and Brandon would ever be a thing.

"Let's go find Blair," I say to Haley.

We go looking everywhere for Blair, but we can't find her. Then I remember something and say, "Come on, let's go back to the old clubhouse. I think that is where Blair went."

"Okay, I mean that makes sense. It is the place we went to get away from Rebecca," Haley says. We head to the old clubhouse and climb the ladder, and sure enough, there is Blair.

"Blair," I say, "is everything alright?"

"No," she replies. "My brother is going out with Rebecca. I mean the one that no one likes. How could he?"

"So it is true then? Is that why you wanted to get away?" I ask.

"Yes, I can't even believe Brandon right now. I mean really, Rebecca. She is terrible. How could he?" Blair says.

"You know what I think? You need a day away from Rebecca. Why don't you and I go on a little adventure? You still haven't seen the town," I say.

"Yes, please. That would be so much fun," Blair says.

"I guess it is settled then. We will get a day away from Rebecca," I say. "You wouldn't mind covering for us, would you?" I ask Haley.

"Oh no, you guys go and have fun. What really matters is Blair," Haley says to me.

Blair and I say goodbye to Haley then head off for Main Street. I show Blair around town, and we do a little bit of shopping. By the time, it is lunchtime; we have been almost everywhere on Main Street. For lunch, we go to the Main Street Diner and have hamburgers.

While we are eating, I say, "So have you enjoyed yourself? I want to take you somewhere special after lunch."

"Ali, this has been one of the best days of my life. Thank you so much especially for getting me away from Rebecca," Blair replies.

"Oh, no problem. Trust me, I know what it is like to want to get away from Rebecca," I say.

We finish eating then I take Blair to, you have probably guessed it by now, my secret place, the weeping willow. It is the best place to go when you need to think, and right now, Blair might need the peace.

I lead Blair into the willow, and she says, "Wow, this place is so cool! How did you find this place?"

"Well let's just say, I had times when I had had enough of Rebecca and needed to get away. I accidentally ran into the branches and found this place, so it is now where I go when I want to get away from Rebecca or when I need to think," I reply.

"Ali, this is awesome. Thank you for showing this to me," she says.

"Oh, no problem. I am just glad that you enjoy it. Feel free to come here whenever you want. Just make sure that you either tell someone in our group or have someone come with you," I say.

After a little while longer, we realize that it is about dinner time, and we should probably head back. Blair says before we go into the house, "Thank you again for the wonderful day. It was awesome!" We eat dinner, and because of such a fun day, I am so tired I finish the dishes fast. I then head upstairs, and as soon as I hit my bed, I am asleep.

Chapter 20

The next morning, I am wakened by Haley and surprisingly not by freezing cold water. I look at my phone and realize it is only 6:00 a.m. "Why did you wake me up so early?" I ask.

"Oh, well," Haley begins as I realize that everyone is already up. "You see we volunteered you to go get groceries."

"That's not so bad, but it still doesn't mean you have to wake me up early," I say.

"No, you don't get it," says Emma.

"You see, we volunteered you to get groceries with—" says Olivia.

"We volunteered you and Brandon to get groceries together at the same time," blurts out Isabelle.

"I still don't see what the problem is," I say. But then I wake up and realize, "You what?"

"We are so sorry, Ali. We didn't think that you and Brandon would be on bad terms. We thought that you guys could work it out before today but apparently not," says Blair.

"Girls, it's fine. You know what, I have been meaning to have a little chat with Brandon after all. I had a few questions for him," I say.

They all look at me like I am nuts or have forgotten that me and Brandon aren't on good terms or that he is with Rebecca. "Girls, it's fine. We can still be friends," I say, wondering if that is a true statement. "Well, I am going back to sleep. See you guys in an hour or two."

I lay down again, and I know exactly what I am going to ask Brandon. An hour later, I wake up, get dressed, and head downstairs for breakfast. During breakfast, Miss Jewel calls out, "Ali and Brandon will be going to the store to get groceries. If anyone else needs anything, they can put it on the list."

After breakfast, I go up to Brandon and ask, "So what time do you want to go to the store?"

"Oh, we can go in a couple of minutes. I just want to grab some things first. Meet you down by the door in about five minutes," he says.

"Sure," I say and head upstairs to get my bag.

Around five minutes later, Brandon and I are ready to go. I grab the list and we start off on our walk to the store. On the way, Brandon says, "Good weather today." The weather really, I think he must really not know what to talk to me about right now.

I reply, "Yes, it is. Brandon, I have a question for you."

He looks surprised but asks, "Okay, what is it?"

"I was just wondering how on earth could you do that to Blair?" I say loudly, trying to contain my anger.

"I'm sorry. I don't understand. What did I do to Blair?" he replies.

"You know, Blair doesn't like Rebecca one bit. Why on earth would you start going out with her? I mean come on, I thought you cared about your sister," I yell, not containing my anger and shouting.

"Well, I am sorry, but she isn't your sister. She is mine, and she will have to deal with whoever I chose to go out with," Brandon shouts back.

"She isn't my sister. You're right but I care for her like a sister. She is like a little sister to me, and I care what happens to her. She was crying yesterday because of it, and I didn't see you go and comfort her. You were probably off with Rebecca. I was with her, and she told me that she never thought that you would do such a thing," I shout back.

"Will you give it a rest? She is my sister, and I can decide who I go out with. It doesn't even involve her," Brandon replies.

"But it has everything to do with her. If you didn't realize, the reason she went off was because Rebecca called her a baby. Rebecca is not respectful, and you will ruin your relationship with your sister if you continue to do this. I can't even believe you! I thought you were different," I say.

We continue to walk toward the grocery store when Brandon says, "What is it with you? You always have to correct what I am doing. Have you ever thought that maybe some people don't like being told what to do?" I am about to shout back when everything suddenly goes all blurry. I can see Brandon falling to the ground too. After that, I don't remember anything.

I wake up to find myself in another place I don't recognize. I see that Brandon is knocked out and that we are tied up. Not again! Of course, we were kidnapped again, and this time, we are in — I see a map on the table that reads Arizona. These people really need to start hiding their maps where they hide us.

I hear footsteps; by this time, Brandon is awake again, but I don't try to talk to him. I see someone coming, and the next thing I know, Brandon and I are being dragged to another separate room. When we get in there and sit down, I hear someone say, "Well, hello, Ali and Brandon. Nice to see you again."

Wait, I know that voice it sounds like Samuel! "Samuel, how did you escape? You are supposed to be in prison," I say.

"Well luckily enough, the officers didn't tie me up right, so I just slipped away while they weren't looking, but I am the one asking the questions here. So where is your sister?" he asks me.

"What are you talking about?" I ask.

"You heard me, where is your sister?" Samuel says.

"I don't have a sister," I reply, very confused.

Samuel replies, "Oh yes, you do!"

The end for now…

About the Author

R achel Rooney wrote this book at age twelve. She has always enjoyed reading, and the next step was writing. This is her first chapter book. She enjoys spending time with her parents and her dog, Sandi.